STAR WARS®

Rey's
Survival Guide

studio fun

A READER'S DIGEST COMPANY

White Plains, New York · Montréal, Québec · Bath, United Kingdom

If you're reading this, then something's gone <u>wrong</u>.

You're stranded on Jakku—a barren little planet with nothing but baking sand, hot sun, and wrecked starships.

Stranded
like me.

My name is Rey.

I've been here my whole life, scratching out a living with the lost and the broken. I don't know how I got here, or why. But I know it was a mistake—and somebody out there will make things right, someday.

That means I need to wait for them. And that means I need to survive.

Self-portrait

That's what I've learned to do on Jakku. I'm writing this to pass the time—and to pass on what I've learned so you have a chance to survive, too.

The only reason anyone's ever heard of Jakku is because a long time ago a lot of people died here. There was a battle fought in space—with ships on fire, plunging out of the skies to lie entombed in the sands.

It's the most important thing that ever happened on Jakku, but that's not saying much. Because as far as I know, it's the <u>only</u> important thing that ever happened on Jakku.

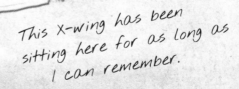

This X-wing has been sitting here for as long as I can remember.

If you ask the people who live here why they do, you'll get a number of answers—_none of them good_.

Pilgrim's Road

Some live here because it is where they were born, and it's all they've ever known. Ask them about other planets, and they'll look at you like you're crazy. Some of them don't know that there's anything beyond the next village—or over that ridge on the horizon.

The INFLICTOR

Some were running from something—the law, or a troubled past, or their own failure to become what they'd wanted to be. They wound up on Jakku because it's about as far as you can go in the galaxy without coming to the end of the stars.

Then there are those who ended up here because of bad luck. They never wanted to stay, but the galaxy had other ideas. And so they wait for something good to happen to them, even though it probably won't, not with all of Jakku's <u>dangers</u>.

They wait. And they <u>survive</u>. I'm going to tell you how to do that.

Before you came to Jakku, I bet you thought it was small and unimportant. And you were right. But up close, every planet is gigantic and full of mysteries—including ones that will kill you. Here's your first survival lesson: <u>Know your surroundings</u>.

I live in the **Goazon Badlands**. It's not really a place, which I know sounds strange, but hear me out. If you ask the locals where the Goazon is, they'll tell you it's between Niima Outpost and the Kelvin Ravine. Or they'll say it's between Carbon Ridge and the Sinking Fields.

Can't say you're in any of those places but know you're somewhere in between them? Then you're in the Goazon.

There isn't much vegetation here—a few spinebarrels in the shadows and maybe a nightbloomer where a bit of dirt's piled up in cracks in the rocks. It's mostly broken land, low hills, and shelves of bare stone that slope down from the heights of Carbon Ridge. As you head away from Carbon Ridge, the Badlands flatten out and the sand builds up until you find yourself crossing into the Sinking Fields.

If you go that far, you've missed the road—which is really just a happabore trail. In Niima they call it the **Pilgrim's Road** because if you follow it eventually you come to the Sacred Villages on the far side of Kelvin Ravine. But I don't remember many pilgrims using it—these days anyone on the road is probably a scavenger heading for the Graveyard of Ships.

Which isn't a good way to find salvation either—but more about that in a bit.

The only real place on the Pilgrim's Road is **Old Meru's**, a shack with a few tables and chairs and a coolth reservoir that went dry before I was born. The cool air's long gone, but there's still shade and a trough for happabores.

Old Meru's

Old Meru is mostly cybernetic parts, and when they cut her up they discarded her ability to make conversation. <u>Don't mess with Meru</u>—the last time someone made that mistake, she came out of her shack with the biggest gun I've ever seen. The sound of her clicking off the safety shut everybody up.

Meru has one flesh-and-blood arm, covered with military tattoos. Don't get caught looking, though—she'll throw you out for being curious. She doesn't like people being curious. Or being anything else.

Tattoos I copied while nobody was looking

I wonder if Meru got those tattoos serving with the Rebellion, the Empire, or some mercenary outfit. I wonder but I don't ask. Like a lot of people on Jakku, Meru doesn't talk about how she got here, and I don't ask. Come to think of it, that's a good second lesson for survival on Jakku:

DON'T ASK.

If you cross the Badlands away from the Pilgrim's Road, you might see Teedos looking for salvage, scavengers coming back from the Graveyard of Ships, bandits hunting prey, or a prospector, pilgrim, hermit, or who knows what.

A Teedo traveler

Most of the time you won't see anybody. And that's for the best.

The Goazon does have a few permanent residents.

My most famous neighbor is the one people know the least about. They call him **the Sitter**. You'll find him near the Pilgrim's Road, almost in the shadow of Carbon Ridge. You can't miss him—he's the only thing visible for kilometers, a hunched figure sitting atop a pillar in the sun.

THE SITTER

The Sitter's human, but I don't know how old he is—he looks skinny and tiny and ancient, dressed in rags bleached by the sun. I bet you'd look that way too if you did what he does.

If you pass by his pillar at sunrise or sunset you might see the Sitter climbing up or down, but otherwise he just sits cross-legged atop his pillar, completely still. As far as I know he's never spoken—certainly he's never said anything to the crazy people who think he's a prophet and stand beneath his pillar asking him questions.

When people bother the Sitter, a Teedo will show up and chase them away. Without the Teedos the Sitter would have died a long time ago. They bring him spinebarrel flesh, nightblossom rind, and water, but as far as I know he never talks to them, either. I don't know why they help him. They're Teedos—sometimes that's the only explanation for what they do.

TEEDOS on their way to the Sitter

CARBON RIDGE

Near the Goazon you'll find **Carbon Ridge**. As you climb it, the wind gets fierce and there are rockslides all the time—set one off and nobody will ever find you at the bottom of the canyon under the tons of stone.

The biggest peril of Carbon Ridge is the **dead-enders**. They sound like a tale from the washing tables, but I've seen them myself, prowling the canyons. They're old men with white beards and crazy eyes. If you run into a dead-ender he'll chase you out of his territory, throwing rocks and babbling nonsense strings of numbers. Fortunately, if they ever had guns they ran out of power packs a long time ago.

There's a story in Niima that somewhere beneath Carbon Ridge the Empire had a base, and the dead-enders are still guarding it.

Is that true?

Well, the dead-enders do wear scraps of old Imperial armor, and something about them does remind me of military types. It's like they're always waiting to come to attention and march off somewhere. You can still see it, underneath all the crazy.

But I don't think there was a base. Why would the Empire have thought twice about this place?

<u>What</u> are they guarding?

Here's what I think happened: In the Battle of Jakku, one of the Empire's warships came down on Carbon Ridge instead of plowing into the Graveyard. The officers that survived sent out stormtroopers to secure the crash site while they waited for a rescue. Instead, they got a rockslide that buried the ship. But the troopers are still there, protecting nothing.

Sounds more likely to me than a secret base.

A word of advice: Don't bring up Carbon Ridge around Unkar Plutt—or the Blobfish, as we call him when he isn't listening.

SINKING FIELDS

When I was just a kid, the Blobfish bought a used flyer that he made me fix—I always could figure out how a machine fit together or why it had broken. I unclogged one of the turbojets and rebuilt the other out of scrap from the front half of an airspeeder. Then off went six of Unkar's thugs with a hired pilot to discover the secret of Carbon Ridge and bring back its buried treasures.

Four of the thugs came back with a stack of stormtrooper armor so brittle that Unkar threw it away. The thugs had shot a handful of dead-enders and lost two of their own in ambushes, but found nothing except empty caves and rockslides. The only life-forms that gained anything were the ripper-raptors of Carbon Ridge—their bellies were full for days.

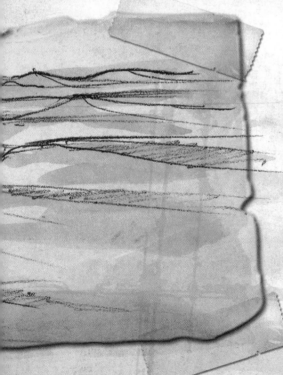

Ever since Unkar's treasure hunt failed, sensible folks leave Carbon Ridge alone.

Go past Pilgrim's Road and you'll wind up climbing ever-higher dunes until they surround you. These are the Sinking Fields, so called because anything that winds up there disappears pretty quickly—the sands just tug things under, and they're never seen again.

This is the walker I turned into a home

Bobbajo the Crittermonger

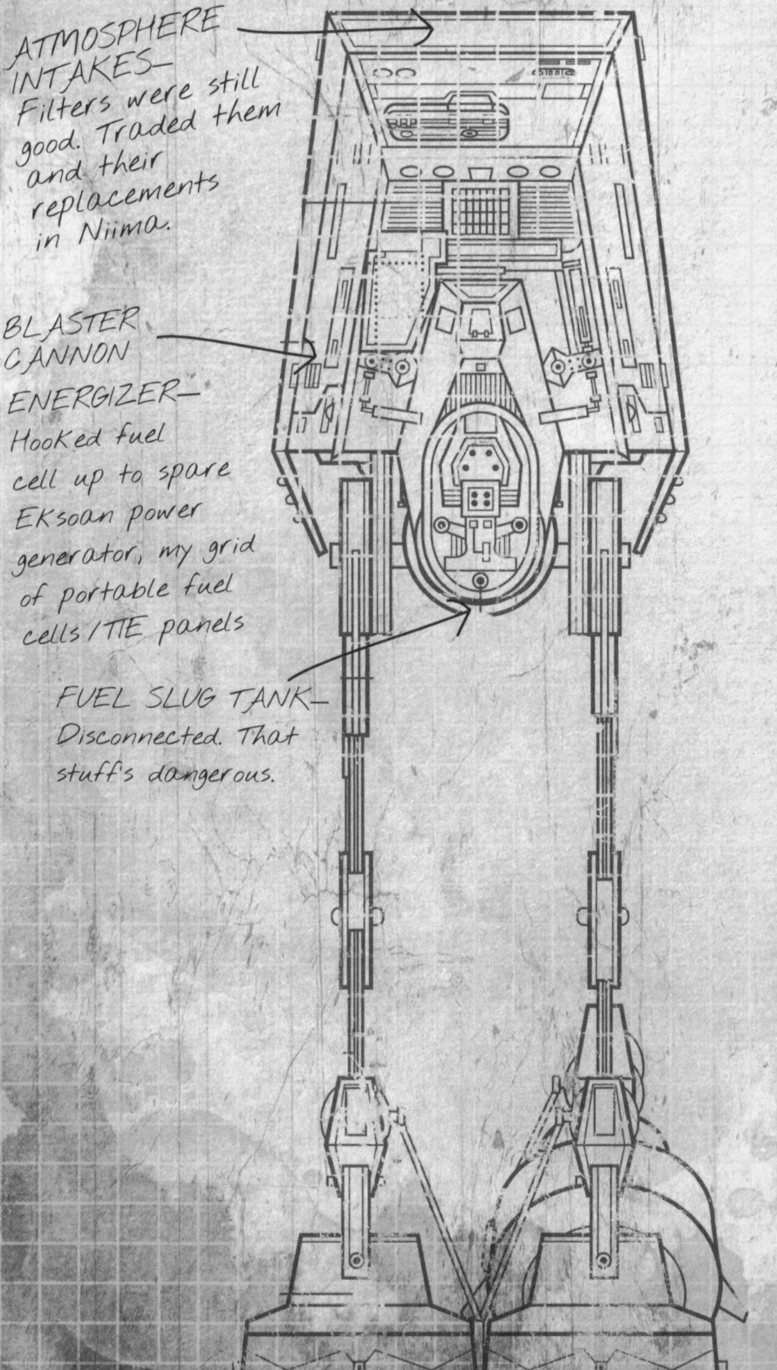

ATMOSPHERE
INTAKES—
Filters were still
good. Traded them
and their
replacements
in Niima.

BLASTER
CANNON

ENERGIZER—
Hooked fuel
cell up to spare
Eksoan power
generator, my grid
of portable fuel
cells/TIE panels

FUEL SLUG TANK—
Disconnected. That
stuff's dangerous.

One of the Sacred Villages. The place gave me the creeps.

Well, unless they reappear—some people claim the Sinking Fields spit things up, too, from walkers to alien ships no one can identify. Except by the time anyone gets out there, the sand's hidden them again.

The Sinking Fields always make me think of an old scavenger named Riok Ragul. Every few weeks, Riok traveled into the Sinking Fields, wearing big flat-sole shoes that spread his weight out and kept him from going under—a Teedo trick, he said.

One day Riok tramped off across the Sinking Fields and didn't return. Some say a nightwatcher worm dragged him under, or he discovered a Teedo secret and they made him disappear.

Maybe.

It's more likely that one of his shoes broke, or his water recycler failed, or he got lost. Or he got caught in one of the storms that last for days, the ones the Teedos call X'us'R'iia, or "the breath of god." <u>A lot can go wrong on foot in the desert</u>.

Travel through the Goazon along the Pilgrim's Road and you'll hit the **Kelvin Ravine**—a gash in the landscape carved by some long-gone river. The road winds its way across the ravine, then climbs up and out to the highlands on the other side where the **Sacred Villages** are.

The people who live there want as little as possible from outsiders—not even goods from the outside world. They've dug their own cisterns, built their own huts, even made their own weapons. I've been out to the Sacred Villages a couple of times, carrying messages from Unkar, but I've never been asked to stay.

In Niima some say the villagers are pacifists, but that's not true. You could ask the bandits who raided the Sacred Villages—except they never came back. You'll find their bones hanging in cages in Kelvin Ravine as warnings.

Different Sacred Villages believe different things. One village believes in the Force and the legends of the old Jedi sorcerers. If that sounds crazy, there's another that thinks the Hutts are gods—cantina talk is that their village is constructed around the cranial mantle of old Niima the Hutt herself, gilded in precious metals and covered with jewels.

Now that's a sight I'd like to see.

TRAVEL ADVISORY

Planet/Star System: JAKKU/Jakku
Warning Level: Red/Proceed With Extreme Caution
Message to spacers approaching Jakku:Captains are advised not to approach Jakku or attempt a landing there.

DETAILS OF HAZARDS:

- The planet is a hostile environment, with extreme temperatures and terrain.
- Services for travelers are minimal to nonexistent, with Jakku's only spaceport (Niima Outpost) classified as a Landing Field.
- Law enforcement capabilities are absent, and extensive reports from Jakku report chronic violations of any recognized rule of Galactic law.
- Commerce on Jakku is rudimentary and controlled by criminal enterprises.
  - Space surrounding Jakku is the site of starship wrecks and unexploded ordnance, posing an active hazard to traffic.

Found this on the Pilgrim's Road.
It's good advice.

I live in a toppled AT-AT walker in the Goazon. It's a strange place, but it's mine. The legs give me a secure place to park my speeder, and cover if I need to get away in a hurry. But I spend most of my time inside the belly.

Instead of a front door, I've got an auxiliary hatch in the underside of the walker. Troops would have used it only in an emergency—they would have entered the side hatch. But I welded that shut a long time ago.

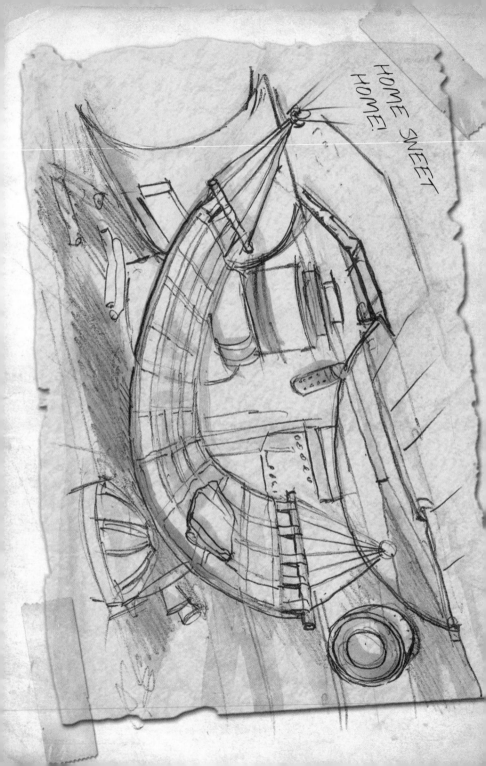

I live inside the lower troop deck. There's a speeder-bike garage and an upper troop deck, but I mostly use just the one room. I don't even think of it as sideways anymore—I've lived here long enough that it feels right this way.

What do I do when I'm home? Mostly, I refurbish gear at my workbench—it costs too much to make extensive repairs at Unkar's washing tables in Niima. I have an old Y-wing computer display I use to study schematics of rebel and Imperial starships and run flight sims. I practice alien languages and droidspeak so I can talk to people in Niima. And I sleep—I made myself a hammock when I was just a kid. At first it was huge, and I would feel lost in the middle of it. Now it fits more snugly.

Dinner is the same thing every night: survival rations. The only variety is whether I get Imperial rations or the New Republic kind. Both are pretty much the same—the New Republic rations taste a bit better but the Imperial stuff is less likely to be stale after all these years.

Unkar trades rations for the gear scavengers salvage from the Graveyard. That's it. No credits, no barter—except for food.

Every night I make a scratch on the wall, marking another day I've survived here on Jakku. Sometimes I think of each mark as a victory—another day where I beat the Blobfish, the heat, and my fellow scavengers. Other times I think of each mark as bringing me closer to the moment when my people return.

I can't tell you how many thousands of times I've eaten this stuff.

Because that will happen one day. I can't tell you when or how, but I know it will—I can feel it. It's a mistake that I wound up here on Jakku, and I know there are people out there who are trying to fix that mistake. When they do, they'll find me and take me to where I belong.

Until that happens, though, I wait.

WARNINGS:

- Vapors released during thermal cooking process are flammable. Do not place an open flame in the vapor, or use in a highly flammable environment.

- Vapors released during thermal cooking process can displace oxygen. Take appropriate precautions.

- If polybag is not prepared properly, expansion of ration may rupture bag and constitute a burn hazard. Edibility of ration may also be adversely affected.

- Water used during thermal cooking process will be hot and constitute a burn hazard. Beware of leaks.

- Do not drink any water remaining in polybag after thermal cooking process or use it in food preparation.

- If consuming ration in prethermal state, do not drink water while chewing, as such actions will initiate the cooking process, resulting in a burn hazard.

- Do not consume polybag, as it has no nutritional value and may constitute a choking and/or digestive hazard.

- Discard polybags after use in accordance with Imperial disposal regulations.

I have a few things at home to help me pass the time. I collect flowers—spinebarrel blooms and nightblossoms—and display them to remind myself that there's beauty everywhere if you look hard enough, even on Jakku.

I have an old rebel
helmet I've kept
around—one of the
first things I ever
found scrounging
the Graveyard.
The name on it
says Captain
Dosmit Raeh of
the Tierfon Yellow

Aces. When I was a kid, I liked to make up stories
about Captain Raeh—about who she was and what
planet she might have come from.

That's why I made a doll out of a flight uniform
I found in a cargo container. I'd put on my helmet
and help Captain Raeh explore the walker and the
sand outside, and together we'd find lost rebels and
get them back to their ships.

I don't do that anymore. But I've
kept these things anyway—to
remind myself of how far
I've come, I guess.

The AT-AT's my home, but my speeder's even more important to my survival. I built it myself, from parts I found in the Graveyard and in junk piles in Niima, along with a few things I got in trade from the Teedos. Everything was stuff I scavenged or that other people had thrown away.

REY'S SPEEDER

inside—2 stacked turbojets

hard day's salvage

My custom speeder: There's nothing like it in the whole galaxy.

I made this fancy schematic like it came out of a factory.

intake ducting (repulsor powered)

My speeder's not easy to pilot. It's top-heavy and if you're not careful, it'll roll. That's fine with me—I know what I'm doing, and if anyone steals my baby they won't get far.

My speeder uses a pair of turbojet engines I took out of a wrecked cargo-hauler. I attached them to amplifier intakes I got out of a crashed Imperial gunship, added afterburners from a racing swoop someone crashed in Niima, then bolted on a bunch of X-wing repulsorlifts.

I designed my speeder to carry heavy loads back and forth between the Graveyard and Niima. But when it's lightly loaded it goes really fast—and pretty high.

The other scavengers don't mess with my ride. One reason is because Unkar's told them not to—not because he likes me but because I bring in the most valuable stuff. The other reason is that I programmed a fingerprint scanner for my speeder. Without that, it won't power up. You could hot-wire it but I intentionally left a wire loose. When I'm exploring a wreck, I attach that wire to the hull and it electrifies the whole thing. It's not enough to kill someone but it will definitely make them think twice about doing that again.

LIFE-FORMS OF JAKKU

Life is tough. Give it a couple of millimeters, even on a forsaken planet like Jakku, and it will figure out the rest.

When I first found my walker, I didn't think I could live there. Everything around it was barren, with no sign of life.

But then I looked closer. And I saw something that amazed me.

There was a little groove on the walker's hip joint where a few millimeters of sand had accumulated. And growing out of that tiny groove was a tiny spinebarrel—a speck of green. I saw that and decided if that little spinebarrel could survive here, so could I.

Whether big or small, life finds a way on Jakku.

The most famous inhabitants of Jakku are the **Teedos**. Nobody knows much about them.

They have scaly gray skin, which you can see above the wrappings they use to keep out the heat, two-fingered hands and a thumb, and feet with two big toes in front and one in the back.

Some people say Teedos evolved here when Jakku had forests and water and other things now lost, and they were tough enough to survive. Others say they came from somewhere else, like the rest of us.

Teedos are pretty smart. Underneath their wrappings is an ingenious system of filters and tubes that reclaims most of their water for recycling. They rig up scanners that can home in on energy signatures. And they can fix almost anything—or take a bunch of parts and build some kind of crazy machine.

They're little, but <u>don't mess with them</u>. Their spears are ionized and can knock you unconscious or even kill you. They'll fight to defend their territory, or over something they think is theirs, or just for some strange Teedo reason.

Still, I've never had a serious problem with the Teedos. I'm pretty good with Teedospeak—I've always been able to figure out how languages work, just like I know machines. And they respect me. They don't mess with my speeder, or act like my home's their territory.

Here's the strangest thing about Teedos: They don't make a distinction between an individual and the group. They don't have names—each of them is just Teedo. Sometimes every Teedo seems to know everything that's happened to every other Teedo, including things no one else witnessed. I don't know how they do that.

A Teedo on a luggabeast

If you meet Teedos in the desert they'll probably be riding on or leading a **luggabeast**. Nobody knows what luggabeasts really look like, because those boxes of armor plating aren't helmets or hats but what they use as heads.

A long walk to Old Meru's

Whoever creates luggabeasts wires their cybernetic systems into their flesh, nerves, and organs. The result is a creature with a lot of endurance, and the ability to detect things with their eyelike scanners. Teedos use the scanners to find electronics, but I've also heard of luggabeasts being used to hunt for water, minerals, or other things.

Luggabeasts are made on some other planet. Occasionally a Teedo comes to Niima Outpost with heads trailing a bundle of wires, and a few weeks later a freighter arrives with more luggabeasts. They come preprogrammed—they just walk down the ramp and go straight to their new masters.

Luggabeasts are small, so larger folks ride **happabores**.

Don't get between a happabore and its water trough.

Happabores have thick skin that lets them shrug off the heat, and they can go for days without water—I've heard from happabore handlers in Niima that they have reservoirs inside their bodies that can store liters of the stuff.

Happabores in motion
are funny things. They
plod along, big snouts
so low to the ground
you fear they'll plow up
sand, and with eyes so tiny
you wonder if they can see
where they're going. But they
trudge along, putting one
big foot in front of the
other, and before you know
it they've covered a lot of
kilometers.

If provoked, happabores can
crush someone with their bite.
But it's pretty hard to provoke
a happabore—they're patient,
obedient, and can take a lot
of abuse.

HAPPY-BORE MEDICATED DEWORMER

(SLURRY FORMULATION)

THE BEST HAPPABORE IS A HAPPY-BORE!

INSTRUCTIONS FOR USE:

Active ingredient: Trestibinexocycline 5-Gamma (1.87%)
Other ingredients: Forage products, thlank oil,
greel-root acid (preservative)

General use instructions: *Using a long-handled*
spatula or related tool, spread Happy-Bore
Medicated Dewormer uniformly on top of the daily
feed ration.

Allow to sit for five standard minutes or until
vapor begins to rise from slurry-feed mixture.

Once vaporization has begun, stir dewormer slurry
vigorously into feed until mixture bubbles.

Summon happabores for daily feeding. Provide
sufficient bunk space so all animals may eat at
same time.

Monitor feeding to ensure properly balanced consumption.

Provide recommended dose of dewormer slurry every nine standard timeparts, adjusting for mean weight of happapore specimens, local parasitic activity, and observed results.

For the removal and control of: bladderworm, crop microserps, multilegged throat croakers, intestinal fangworm colonies, lesser and greater nasal nesting spit-crawlers, cranial nodular worms.

Not recommended for control of: flesh-eating daggerworms (Trenwyth), brain crawlers (Cheelit), Maxilan's explosive bloatworm (Lanteeb).

STORE AT AMBIENT TEMPERATURE WITHIN MANUFACTURER'S PARAMETERS. MUST BE MIXED BEFORE FEEDING ACCORDING TO DIRECTIONS.

WARNING: IN RARE CASES, SICKNESS MAY OCCUR AFTER DOSING IN BREEDING MALES EXPERIENCING MUSTH AFTER DOSING. THIS IS A NORMAL REACTION. IF ANY BODILY FLUID COMES IN CONTACT WITH SKIN, FLUSH IMMEDIATELY WITH ALKALINE SOLUTION AND SEEK PROFESSIONAL ATTENTION TO AVOID PERMANENT STAINING OF DERMAL LAYERS AND RETENTION OF ODOR.

"THE BEST HAPPABORE IS A HAPPY-BORE!"

DISTRIBUTED BY GALACTI-STOK,
A SUBSIDIARY OF TAGGECO

When happabores come into Niima from a long jaunt along the Pilgrim's Road, you'll find them in the center of town at one of the big water troughs. They'll drink for the better part of forever, sticking out big tongues and sucking up water until those mysterious reservoirs are filled up.

A handler once told me there are happabores on a lot of planets out here in the Western Reaches, and they do everything from pulling plows and ice sledges to carrying around princes and princesses. That's another thing I'd like to see—happabores pulling a carriage filled with royalty. The happabores would be well cared for, with as much clean water as they wanted to drink, fodder to eat, and a cool pen out of the sun.

Sounds like a good life.

Bloggins are avians with eyestalks and long tails. Their eyestalks let them see predators coming from far away, but this doesn't do much good because they might be the dumbest creatures in the galaxy. Their reaction to trouble is to panic, run around in circles squawking, and then try to fly (which they aren't very good at).

The Sacred Villagers raise bloggins for meat, feathers, and oil. And if you're in Niima, Bobbajo the Crittermonger will have some trussed for sale on his back.

One creature I hate seeing is the **steelpecker**. They're nasty avians with razor-sharp beaks and iron-hard talons. You'll find them roosting inside the wreckage of the Graveyard, where they hunt for rare alloys and metals.

You can shoo away a lone steelpecker, but one of the worst things I ever saw happened when a scavenger named Teng Malar accidentally broke open a hatch below a steelpecker colony. They came from every direction and there was nothing I could do—within ten minutes they'd ripped Teng to shreds.

Steelpeckers search for vanadium, osmiridium, and corundum, which they store in their gizzards. So you want to <u>stay away</u> from parts with concentrations of those— such as gyroscopic equipment or focusing arrays that have been exposed to intense heat.

You'll mostly find **ripper-raptors** up on Carbon Ridge or in the Kelvin Ravine. They're reptilian, with leathery wings and keen eyesight, and spend their days riding the thermals, looking for carrion. If you see ripper-raptors circling a spot on Jakku, you know someone or something there is in <u>trouble</u>.

If ripper-raptors see you, don't stop.

If you're hurt in the desert and the ripper-raptors don't get you, the **gnaw-jaws** will. These bugs are about a third of a meter long—with chitinous plates, too many legs, and big scissor-like mandibles. They live in warrens of tunnels beneath the sand, coming out at night. They generally avoid people but they'll take advantage of someone who's weak or asleep. If you're forced to camp in the desert, a circle of powdered barium will keep them away.

Nightwatchers—some locals call them sandborers or Arconan night terrors—mostly stick to the Sinking Fields, though supposedly they can migrate into the Goazon when big storms push sand dunes that way. They're massive worms, twenty meters long when fully grown, with some specimens five or six times that size.

Devi and Strunk once told me they were crossing the Sinking Fields at night and saw a nightwatcher that could have swallowed Niima. But I don't believe that. Because those two swindlers have told me a lot of things.

I've heard nightwatchers hunt by sensing vibrations above them, erupting out of the Sinking Fields with their jaws open to engulf whatever they find. They aren't choosy, because there's nothing a nightwatcher can't devour. Their mouthparts can grind metal into scrap, and their stomachs generate acid to melt down anything they can't digest.

Just one more reason to stay out of the Sinking Fields.

THE GRAVEYARD OF SHIPS

You'll run into people on Jakku who say they were there when the ships fell out of the sky. They're either lying or crazy. The Battle of Jakku was before there was a Niima Outpost or much of anything else on this miserable planet. So unless you've gained magical powers and are talking to a ripper-raptor or a nightwatcher worm, they probably weren't there.

No one on Jakku knows exactly how all those ships came down in the desert. The story that makes the most sense to me is the Empire made a last stand here, and their commanders tried to take as many enemy ships as they could with them.

Why does that make sense? Because any scavenger with a brain (which is by no means all of us) can tell you that every Imperial ship out in the Graveyard shows considerable battle damage—burned-out shield generators, hull armor pierced or melted by laser fire, blast points from concussion missiles and proton torpedoes.

That's true of a lot of the New Republic ships, too—but not all, and that's the strange thing. There are New Republic ships that show crash damage but nothing else.

Weird, right?

There's an explanation you'll hear at the Niima washing tables that I think might actually be true: When the Imperial captains realized they were beaten, they locked on to the nearby New Republic warships with their tractor beams and pulled them down into Jakku's gravity well. So everything wound up in pieces in the Graveyard of Ships—Imperial capital ships, New Republic cruisers, fighters, you name it.

That explains the damage you see, but why would anybody do such a thing?

Take your pick of the stories you'll hear around the washing tables:

Theory 1

It was to protect that secret Imperial base I told you about, the one under the Carbon Ridge.

Theory 2

No, the Imperial base was beneath the Sinking Fields. And it wasn't a base, but a storehouse filled with treasure looted from ancient civilizations and hidden on Jakku by the Emperor.

Theory 3

That's close, but not quite right. See, the Emperor had a throne room here, from which he planned to explore and conquer the rest of the galaxy.

You get the idea. It gets real crazy real fast. Someday some scavenger at the washing tables is going to look around to make sure no one's listening and then swear up and down that the Emperor was really a Teedo, and he came here to spend his retirement fixing old droids while sitting on the back of his favorite luggabeast.

Whatever the reason, the fact is that the Empire and the New Republic fought here, above Jakku. And when they were done fighting, the Graveyard of Ships was left behind.

The Graveyard is where most of the ships came down, but not all of them. You'll find wrecked fighters in Kelvin Ravine, blown-apart engine nacelles littering Carbon Ridge, and bits of metal and trash from one end of the Goazon to the other. Ships came down everywhere on Jakku, including places people have never thought to look.

Most of the people aboard those ships died the second they hit the ground—a fall from orbit will do that. Sounds bad, but they were the lucky ones.

The ones who made it to an escape pod or ejected from a fighter came down in the middle of a desert with survival gear meant to keep you alive long enough to walk to the nearest settlement. Back then the nearest settlement was a dozen or so light-years away. So they died of exposure wandering the Goazon, or lay down in a cave to starve to death, or grew too weak to shoo the ripper-raptors away.

The Graveyard's full of bodies, from Feressee's Point to the Spike. Some of those big Imperial ships had populations a lot larger than all of Jakku, which means _a lot of bones_.

I don't really notice the bones anymore—there are simply too many of them. These days I only think about them when I come across a body that's more or less intact. Like the TIE pilot I found just outside the Crackle, still strapped into his ejector seat. I found him because I saw the rags of his parachute above him, whipping this way and that in the wind.

I took the pilot's helmet, sidearm, and comlink, along with his ejector seat's gyros and magnetic couplings— all that stuff's valuable in Niima, and it wasn't going to do him any good. Then I buried him, still in his uniform.

SHIPS OF THE GRAVEYARD

Nebulon-B Frigates

Y-wings

Calamari Cruisers

TIE Fighters

A-wing Fighters

Blockade Runners

Star Destoyers

-X-wings

B-wings

I know about all the ships you'll find in the Graveyard—what roles they played in combat, what weapons they carried, even their starship models and classes and how many crew members they had.

I learned that stuff by exploring wrecks and pulling systems apart and putting them back together, and by studying schematics and maintenance data-tapes and astromech memory cores.

I've never seen an Imperial command shuttle's hyperdrive generator, but I know the manual for it by heart. Give me one and I could get the shuttle running in ten minutes—and I could fly it, too. I've flown lots of ships, at least by simulator. And one real ship, for a little while—a Ghtroc 690 freighter. But I don't want to talk about that.

If you're going to survive here, you need to know about the ships you'll find in the Graveyard, the _valuable parts_ they contain, and the _dangers_ they present.

A-wing fighters—good luck finding one of these that's salvageable. Nearly all the ones I know of are just shredded metal. Too bad—I've read the pilot's manual for this little New Republic fighter, and it looks like it was faster than a luggabeast chased by a steelpecker flock.

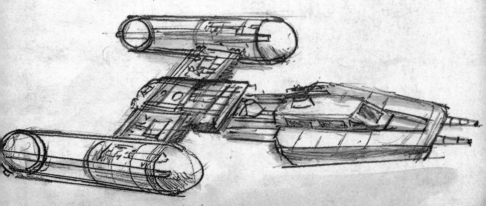

Y-wing fighters—they built these fighters to last, and some are in pretty good shape considering what they came through. Be careful of the proton-torpedo launch racks beneath the cockpit. Check if the sensor domes are still attached to the turbine engines—if they're gone, the Y-wing's probably been stripped already.

Mon Calamari
Cruisers—these
bulbous ships were
New Republic craft, and
no two are exactly alike. They
look a bit like spinebarrels with a
fungal disease, covered with bulges. Some of the
bulges are actually detachable ships—a decade ago
a scavenger named Porvay Yan discovered a shuttle
that still could fly and traded it for a ticket off
this rock. The issue with Mon Cal ships is that
they weren't made for other species, so few of their
components can be salvaged.

Nebulon-B
frigates—crash
damage has
reduced most of
these angular
ships to scrap—
the boom
connecting the
engines and forward section is
pretty fragile, and the same goes
for the outrigger beneath the bow.
It's pretty rare to find a Nebulon-B
left with anything of value.

TIE fighters—I find these fighters interesting. They've got some really advanced gear but they're pretty cheaply made, without shield generators or hyperdrives, or anything better than basic life-support functions. Strange...I thought the Empire was the one with all the credits back then.

Blockade runners—
another tough ship. Many
came down relatively intact,
but it's rare to find one with
escape pods still attached. I suspect
they all ejected on the way down.

X-wing fighters—
you'll find these New
Republic fighters scattered
around the Graveyard, most looking
like they were brought down by
surface-to-
air fire or
atmospheric dogfights. You can get a clue to
what happened to these fighters based on whether
the ejection seat's inside or not.

Variant TIE models—there are valuable components in both the bat-winged fighters and the bombers with twin pods. Careful around the bombers, though—their proton bombs are pretty unstable after so many years. A while back a scavenger named Namenthe was driving a speeder full of salvaged proton bombs and two smacked into each other a little too hard. The site's now called <u>Namenthe's Crater</u>.

B-wing fighters—scavengers talk about these heavy New Republic fighters a lot—they're filled with components that would bring a lot of credits in Niima. Unfortunately, the few I've seen with my own eyes came down hard and then were looted early. And I've never seen a B-wing cockpit— apparently they doubled as escape pods.

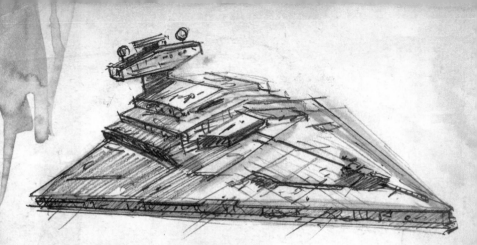

Imperial Star Destroyer—these huge ships were the main battleships of the Empire, and most were shot to pieces by the time they came down on Jakku. The ones that landed top-down are pretty much demolished, but you'll find others sitting upright in the sand. One of the most intact Star Destroyers is the Inflictor. Squatters live in her conning towers, chasing away anyone who invades their territory.

You'll find other craft in the Graveyard, of course—Imperial shuttles, walkers, New Republic transports, and wrecks so busted up that no one can identify them. And of course there are rumors about ships we've never seen, ones buried in the sand that will reappear when the dunes let them go someday. I've heard scavenger tales about New Republic command ships filled with credits for new planetary governments, Imperial battlecruisers reconfigured as hyperspace explorers, and even stranger stuff. Which means people will be scouring the Graveyard for centuries after I'm gone.

Supposedly this crashed Super Star Destroyer was known as the **Ravager**.

These Super ships were so much bigger than regular Destroyers.

Most of the ship shattered on impact, but the back section lies belly-up in the Graveyard. Over the years, the Super's been stripped pretty thoroughly by scavengers and is mostly a hollowed-out shell. Rumor has it her command decks survived the impact and are mostly intact, down there beneath the sand. I kind of doubt that, but who knows.

Engineering station.

Engineering station has been exposed but is worth a look.

Drive unit capacitor banks

Ion accelerator chambers

A lot of the hull armor has been removed to get at underlying systems.

Scroungers have hollowed out most of the main drive array and reactor housing forward of it.

Imperial Super Star Destroyer—I only know of one of these monstrous ships in the Graveyard, but she's truly gigantic, with the back section alone bigger than a regular Star Destroyer. The Super-flight logs from other Imperial craft identify her as the **Ravager**—came down bow-first, like someone threw a spear at Jakku.

Power trunking for ion accelerators

Sublight engines

Main drive engines

Neutrino radiators

Is the tower and bridge intact beneath all that sand? Seems unlikely.

Careful—various laser-brains I could name may have cracked the reactor or opened fuel lines.

SCAVENGER'S SURVIVAL TIPS

MASHR,
(I miss her.

I've been a scavenger as long as I can remember. I worked for others at first, climbing into ducts and conduits too small for grown-ups. Some of the scavengers I helped were kind, like Ivano Troade and Mashra. Others—whose names I won't mention—thought I was their property.

I was still very young when I realized that I knew how to scavenge and survive on Jakku better than any of them. They needed me, but I didn't need them. So I struck out on my own.

At first nobody took me seriously. But I had help, even though I didn't want it—Unkar Plutt told the others to leave me alone and sent his thugs to make the other scroungers back off.

Me—geared up for maximum protection

Once I built my speeder, I had my independence. Not _real_ independence, of course. There's no such thing on Jakku—Unkar controls everything. But while I'm here I can go where I want, when I want.

Though mostly that means I go to the Graveyard. Because I have to.

The biggest danger in the Graveyard is one scavengers don't think about enough—heat. You become dehydrated, your body temperature climbs, and you don't think straight when something goes wrong. That means making a bad decision, which means you die. Paos Adina, Turgot Mynes, Binz Scoty—the list of scavengers who messed up and died of the heat is a long one. I'm not adding my name to it.

To keep the heat off, I wear
<u>wrappings</u> and <u>sun goggles</u>.
I always have much <u>more</u>
<u>water than I need</u> and
<u>replacement parts</u> for
everything critical on my
speeder. And I leave any
wreck site <u>ninety minutes</u>
before I think I should—
even if I think I'm just
moments from being able to
salvage something
Unkar Plutt will pay
handsomely for.

That means I've lost out on
valuable gear and had to take
less in trade from the Blobfish. But
to quote Mashra, **nobody will pay
you if you're dead.**

Another big hazard is <u>injuries</u>. It's dark
inside the dead ships, and you can run
into jagged metal that will slice you open
or step on hull plating that's turned
brittle and is the only thing between
you and a hundred-meter drop. If I'm
somewhere new I don't hurry and use my
staff to check that every step is stable.

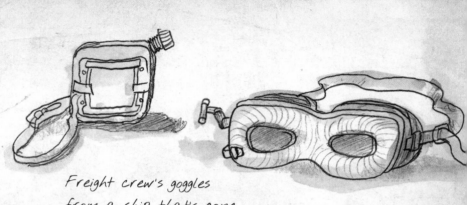

Freight crew's goggles
from a ship that's gone.

I've heard of scavengers who walked into something
sharp and cut their own throats, or fell into
abysses beneath the Graveyard. But most fatal
injuries aren't so dramatic. If you've climbed fifty
meters down into a Star Destroyer's hangar and
then trip on a length of conduit and break your
wrist, you won't be able to climb out again. It
seems crazy that a broken wrist could kill you,
but it can.

The majority of power systems in the Graveyard
ran out of charge a long time ago, but you need
to be careful around TIE fighters—a lot of their
solar panels are still collecting power. Varè
Malago died when he stepped on the loose end of
some TIE bomber power trunking—it was beneath a
couple of centimeters of sand but left him burning
like a torch.

Radiation will kill you if you're not careful, and so will corrosive fuel. And liquid coolant can vaporize and displace the oxygen in a space, leaving you with nothing to breathe.

You can tell dangerous fuel by colors in the sand. Rhydonium looks like spilled chrome, and can be scraped up and salvaged—but don't touch it with bare skin. Green sand means **barium**, which is poisonous and should be handled carefully. If you see purple or red sand, back up. That's rubidium or strontium, and even breathing it can kill you.

FUEL: baradium, baradium nitrate, nergon-14, megonite

Gold: iron

Purple: rubidium

Green: barium

Red: strontium

Chrome: rhydonium

Blue: copper

Orange: calcium

Yellow: sodium

Then there's the threat of other scavengers. I have a reputation in Niima Outpost for being willing to use my staff, which keeps most of the riffraff from bothering me. Still, there are always new scavengers who don't know the rules, or are desperate enough not to care. I keep my ears open in Niima so I know who might do something stupid. I try to avoid those scavengers but if it comes to it, I'm not arguing with a blaster. Anyone operating that way in the Graveyard isn't going to last much longer anyhow—they'll make a mistake and stop being a problem.

Let's assume you don't get shot, cut yourself open, fall in a pit, or die of exposure to heat, poison, or radiation. In that case, you'll need to know which components will get you the most in trade at Niima Outpost.

Gear is most valuable if it can be reused in other starships, vehicles, building systems, or droids. The barrel of a Star Destroyer turbolaser is an impressive piece of hardware—but unless you know a crazy person building his own Star Destroyer, it's worthless in Niima. (And good luck dragging it across the desert.)

What you want to salvage are pumps, filters, impellers, valves, pistons, fuel injectors, inverters, capacitors, and bearings. All that stuff can be reused in most anything.

Also look for data conduits, cooling shunts, and fuel piping. A lot of that material is flexible and can be coiled up for transport. But watch out for pooled coolant or fuel—it can be volatile, poisonous, or both.

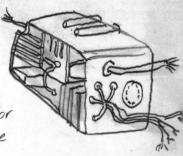

Batteries and power cells are both valuable and still pretty common in the Graveyard. They powered blasters, droids, comlinks, turbolasers, communications gear, sensor arrays, and everything else. Your tester wi tell you if a cell can be recharged.

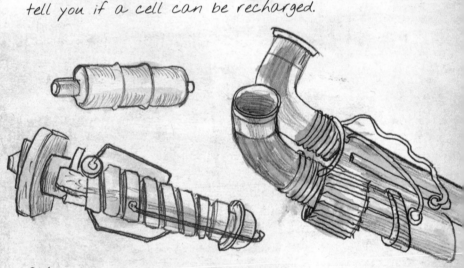

Other common things to look for are sensor arrays, landing lights, subspace radios, and power converters. And don't forget items that have nothing to do with space combat, such as first-aid kits, water filters, and portable heaters. Field rations are fine as long as they're sealed.

Most military hardware isn't as useful as you might think, but UnKar will trade for sensor arrays, shield projectors, tractor-beam emitters, and transponders. Blasters always sell. There are folks in Niima who'll happily take an E-Web blaster or other heavy weaponry.

It's pretty rare to find a droid worth salvaging in the Graveyard—most of them were taken years ago. If it happens, it's your lucky day because <u>nearly all droids are valuable</u>. There are tinkerers in the bazaar who can get them running again, or else they can be broken down for the parts box. Power droids, load lifters, and astromechs are the most in demand on JakKu.

As a scavenger, your tools are your life. Here's what's in my satchel:

* set of Pilex bit drivers, with Wessex and Blissex heads
* bag of quick-switch modulars, including everything from Mon Calamari hex-clamps to cruciform Verpine ratchets
* hydrospanners in all eight standard configurations, with spare power cells
* magnetizer and demagnetizer
* carbon chisel for removing scoring from parts, and a vibro-model for really tough jobs

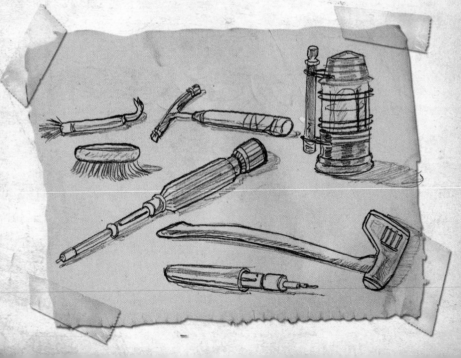

* chisel head hammer

* Harris wrenches, two powered and one standard

* bonding tape

* power tester

* microlenses to check for tiny breaks and cracks

* sensor jammer for decoupling memory units and computers so they don't purge their data when unhooked without authorization

* datapad loaded with schematics

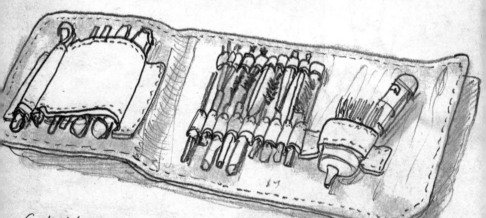

Get the best tools you can, learn to use them, and maintain them properly.

A valuable thing scavengers overlook is <u>information</u>. The scrounger Miggs McKane retired to Ogem after he sliced his way into the data core of a Star Destroyer and found a complete Imperial order of battle, which he eventually sold to some off-worlder. At least that's the story they tell in Niima.

To find the most valuable equipment, you need to know ship schematics backward and forward—that will keep you from spending hours poking around blindly and getting hurt.

Miggs
McKane

The turbolaser turrets of an Imperial Star Destroyer are hooked to large arrays of <u>auxiliary power cells</u>—just follow the power trunking. I don't mess with the power core—or anything related to the reactor—but conduits lead from it throughout the ship and can be salvaged. The bridge and the officers' quarters below it are good places to look for datapads, droids, comlinks, and the like. Up near the bow you'll find <u>liquid stores</u> and holds for raw materials.

Most systems aboard a Mon Calamari Cruiser will be hard to adapt for use, but check on the deflector-shield generators amidships. They're surrounded by conduits and auxiliary power cells that can be extracted. The <u>sensor arrays</u> and <u>communications suites</u> in the bow are valuable and relatively easy to move.

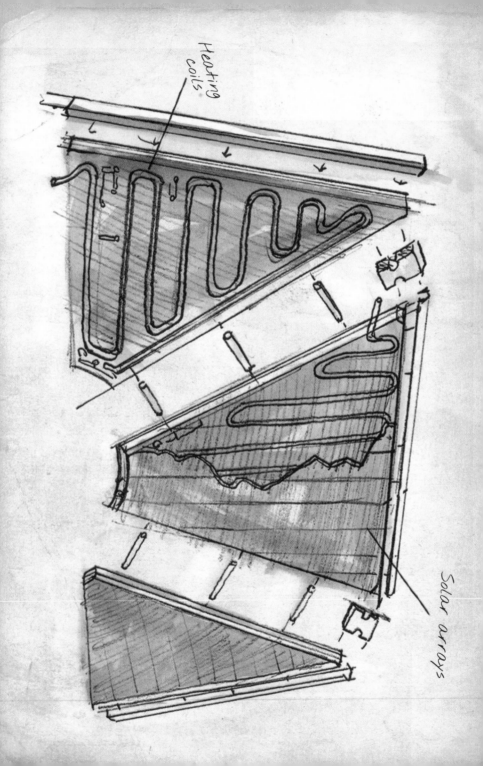

Heating coils

Solar arrays

With a Nebulon-B frigate, the dorsal shield generator is a big array of linked generators, with power cells that are reasonably well protected. And check the chief engineer's quarters—when I was a kid I found schematics for four different models of the New Republic starfighter in a datapad.

When I find a TIE fighter, the first thing I do is look at the solar arrays—each wing has six, with energy accumulator lines running back and forth beneath the solar panels. If you find an array that's undamaged or mostly intact, it can be salvaged. If not, the power lines and energy coils are worth taking.

The most valuable parts of a Y-wing are the sensor arrays beneath the domes on each of the engine outriggers. The turbines are valuable, too—but if you crack the reactors forward of them you'll be swallowing rad pills for weeks. In the main body of the fighter are two power cells, power generators, and a coolant pump.

If you actually find an intact A-wing, you want the shield generators, the swivel mounts for the laser cannons, and the forward sensor arrays. A-wings were built for speed, so the power generators, trunking, and waste-heat radiators are all specially reinforced.

With X-wings, I move aft from the bow, grabbing the sensor array out of the nose and then looking for an intact sensor computer, communications antenna, and flight computer. Don't miss the <u>repulsorlifts</u>—I scavenged a bunch of those for my speeder. Behind the pilot's seat, you'll find power converters and trunking to the generator. The wings have power couplings, heat sinks, and other stuff you can grab. Don't forget the <u>cargo bay</u>—the New Republic trained its pilots in survival, so there's often useful gear in there.

Intact B-wings are even rarer than A-wings, but full of interesting gear. The main sensor array and long-range scanners are located where the wings meet. You'll find <u>high-efficiency power cells</u> in the two lateral wings, along with repulsorlift projectors. Working up toward the cockpit (almost certainly gone), you'll find the shield generators and the four engine nozzles. Just don't jostle the reactors or the torpedo magazine. Finally, the <u>magnetic couplings</u> that once held the cockpit in place are easy salvage in Niima.

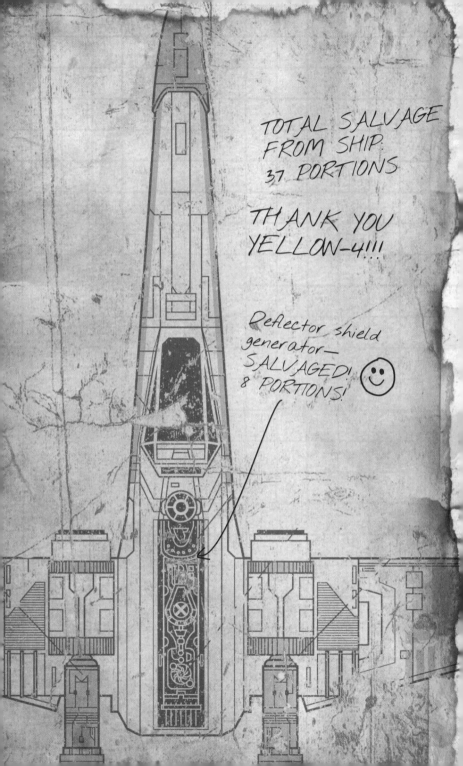

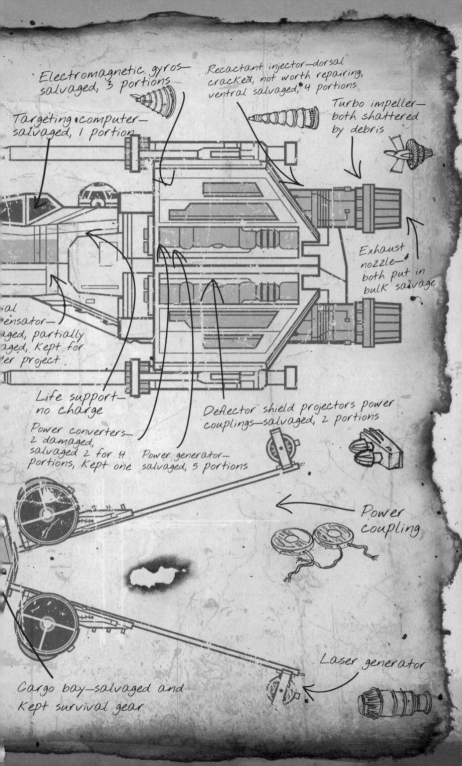

Electromagnetic gyros—
salvaged, 3 portions

Reactant injector—dorsal
cracked, not worth repairing,
ventral salvaged, 4 portions

Turbo impeller—
both shattered
by debris

Targeting computer—
salvaged, 1 portion

Exhaust
nozzle—
both put in
bulk salvage

ial
ensator—
aged, partially
aged, kept for
er project

Life support—
no charge

Deflector shield projectors power
couplings—salvaged, 2 portions

Power converters—
2 damaged,
salvaged 2 for 4
portions, kept one

Power generator—
salvaged, 5 portions

Power
coupling

Laser generator

Cargo bay—salvaged and
kept survival gear

Cockpit—ejector seat fired, removed cockpit controls for speeder

Sensor computer—trashed

Communications antenna—repaired, 3 portions

Primary sensor array—broken, can't be salvaged

Canopy—missing (ejected)

Nose cone—broken in crash

...nergy sensor jammer unit—...lvaged, 4 portions ...om the Blobfish

Repulsorlifts—removed for speeder project

Inert comp... salv... dam... speed...

...light computer—capacitors ...nd memory drive salvaged, ...2 portions, transponder ID says ...fighter was Yellow-4 (Tierfon)

Hydraulic lines (landing gear)—salvaged, 1 portion, also removed pistons, pivot (bulk salvage)

Port wing laser cannons—both snapped off in crash

Hyperdrive—slagged, some components for bulk salvage

Note: there are four wings, engines, and laser cannons***

NIIMA OUTPOST

Here's an ironclad rule of surviving as a scavenge

All salvage is worthless until you've been paid for it.

Here's another rule: **Don't talk about salvage.** It can take a couple of days to remove all the salvageable gear from an X-wing, so keep your lips zipped until it's a chassis full of sand. Even then, don't talk—because if you found something good, the might be something else good out that way.

Once you get to Niima, you're in the domain of **Unkar Plutt, the Blobfish.**

I have my own tools and speeder, but no full cleaning rig—and no way of getting one. So, the fir thing I do in Niima is head to Unkar's washing tables. The cost of renting a table comes out of t final trading price, so make sure your salvage is in the best possible shape before you arrive—it's ba business paying Unkar for time getting sand out or a fuel pump.

The Washing Tables

Unkar pays more for working salvage than he does for gear that he has to repair, so whatever you bring him has to be functional. If you can, fix it yourself. But sometimes that isn't possible.

If that's the case, tinkerers in the bazaar will recharge gear or let you poke through their replacement parts. Not for free, of course—nothing on Jakku is free except heat—but they'll make a better deal with you than Unkar will.

My favorite tinkerer is Lerux Talley, a scrawny little human who says he's from the Core Worlds, which probably isn't true. If I need welding, I see a manumitted power droid named AMPS. AMPS doesn't eat rations, of course, but he'll weld in exchange for a recharge, spare gas canisters, metals he finds interesting, or a good joke. I spend a lot of time driving across the Goazon trying to think of jokes AMPS will decide are worth a trade.

AMPS (EGL-21)

Unkar sits in the concession stand—that's what we call his stronghold in the center of Niima. It's an old cargo crawler, but the Blobfish has outfitted it with security monitors and hidden defenses—not to mention he always has his goons around, and they'll beat up anybody who dares to cross him.

The Blobfish sits behind his barred window all day, examining junk, muttering to himself, and yelling at his goons as if he's afraid that we scavengers would tear him apart if he set one blobby foot outside.

Another
self-portrait

Unkar has power because he controls the food supplies on Jakku, which consist almost completely of survival rations his goons took out of the Graveyard. If you want to eat, you have to find junk to bring to Unkar in exchange for food.

It's a bad situation, but I remember that my being here is a mistake. And when that mistake gets fixed, I'll wave good-bye to Unkar, Niima Outpost, and Jakku.

There isn't much to Niima beside the Blobfish's concession stand, particularly if you don't have credits. There's the bazaar where you can buy guns and black-market stuff, and a couple of launch bays that pass for a spaceport. But nothing anyone leading a normal life would want.

The spacers who come here sleep aboard their ships. For food, there's whatever they brought or what they can buy from Bobbajo the Crittermonger. No one knows why, but Unkar allows Bobbajo to sell food—but only to spacers, not to us scavengers.

How can the Blobfish get away with this? Because he controls everything in Niima—including the muscle.

That's the way it's always worked going back to Niima the Hutt, who was the first to put a beacon in the desert. Niima ran Jakku until a bounty hunter shot her down. Since then, the Blobfish has operated by the same principle of might makes right.

The Blobfish's thugs keep their faces hidden while they work, which I've always found funny. Mast Surko's the only person on this planet with a black

metal cybernetic leg.
I call Mast by name
whenever I see him in
Niima, holding his vibro-
ax and bumping into
things because he's
wearing his silly
hood. First he looks
around like he's
confused, then he
hurries away with
the servomotors
whining in his leg.

Then there's
Sarco—he's not
one of Unkar's,
but a bounty
hunter or
something. I don't
mess with him. There's
a rumor he killed a
squad of stormtroopers
on a jungle planet
once. Don't know
if that's true, but
he's certainly mean
enough.

Sarco Plank

The closest thing we've got to law and order in Niima is Constable Zuvio. You'll see him under his big Kyuzo helmet, with his fellow self-proclaimed guardsmen. Zuvio and his men are decent enough, actually—they step in when the Blobfish's thugs get too rowdy. But like everybody else on Jakku, they work for Unkar and they know it.

The folks I wonder about most in Niima are the visitors.

Some of them are traders doing business with Unkar—he doesn't have a reliable starship these days, so his customers mostly come to him. Others are prospectors making a last stop before heading off into the Unknown Regions.

Constable Zuvio

But every now and then I see people in Niima who shouldn't be here—families standing at the bottom of starship ramps, peering out in disbelief at the bazaar and the endless sand. They're the ones I worry about and try to watch out for. Is that how I got here—because someone just passing through made a terrible mistake?

I have to stay, but they don't. So it's always a relief to see those strange ships lift off again.

ADDENDUM

I always thought this guide would wind up in the hands of someone else trying to survive on Jakku. But if you're reading this, you know things changed.

I barely know how to begin, because the last couple of days have been astonishing.

My first glimpse of BB-8

It started with this droid—an astromech but one of the newer ones, not the kind you find in the Graveyard. I'd finished dinner when I heard him near the house, beeping for all he was worth.

A Teedo had him caught in a net. I didn't care for that—this was right by my house, which the Teedos know isn't their territory. I needed to show them I wouldn't put up with that, or else I'd soon have the same problem with every Teedo on Jakku.

I yelled at the Teedo and cut the droid out of the net. I wondered if the Teedo would try to zap me with his staff, but he gave up and rode off on his luggabeast.

The droid said his name was **BB-8**. His antenna was bent, so he couldn't contact whomever he'd been with and get back to wherever he'd come from. He tried to tell me about it but my droidspeak isn't perfect, so I couldn't figure out what he was saying.

I could tell BB-8 would be worth a lot of rations, but I couldn't bear the idea of turning him over to the Blobfish. Someone would be looking for him, and something told me it was important that he be found—and by the right people.

If I could have fixed his antenna I would have, and then everything would have been different. Since I couldn't, I told him he could spend the night in my home, and then we'd go to Niima in the morning. I figured he could get a ride from there.

When I woke up I thought it was all a dream— like the green planets I only get to see in my sleep. But it was real. I took BB-8 to Niima and told him to ask the trader in Bay 3 for a ride. But he wouldn't leave—he said he was waiting for someone.

That got to me a bit, I admit.

I didn't know what to do, so I brought some gear I'd fixed the night before over to the Blobfish. When Unkar saw the droid, he got this crazy look in his eyes. The next thing I knew, he was offering me _sixty portions_ for him.

The Blobfish

I'm not proud of what I did next, but see it from my perspective. You can eat for <u>a month</u> on sixty portions—longer if you stretch it. And if I kept finding good scores in the Graveyard, I could keep those rations in reserve—or sell them for credits.

Credits would mean freedom from the Blobfish.

I asked for a hundred portions and Unkar agreed immediately. That's how I knew I'd messed up.

I told him the droid wasn't for sale. That made him angry. Then I told him conditions had changed. Because how many times had the Blobfish said the same thing when he decided to go back on a deal?

But that was a bigger mistake. Because now Unkar was angry—angry enough to forget I'm his best scavenger.

There's a scrounger in Niima named Crusher Roodown. For years he was one of the Blobfish's best scavengers, but he got into a dispute with the Blobfish, and Unkar sent his thugs to cut off Crusher's arms.

Crusher does odd jobs around Niima for half-rations now, which is how I know the Blobfish regrets what he did—otherwise he would have had Crusher killed. But Unkar feeling bad won't help Crusher any. He's stuck with aftermarket mechanical arms and will never salvage anything again.

All the talk in Niima has been about an attack on Tuanul, one of the Sacred Villages, on the other side of Kelvin Ravine: supposedly **First Order** stormtroopers had torched the place, looking for something.

It didn't take a lot for me to put two and two together. BB-8 was connected to whatever had happened out there. Which almost certainly meant he was a Resistance droid. Which meant the First Order would be looking for him. Which meant they'd torch Niima, just like the Sacred Village.

When Unkar's thugs showed up and told me they were taking the droid...well that wasn't going to happen.

Unkar's thugs are big and mean, but they're used to people who are too scared to fight back. That's never described me and _never will_.

I thrashed them, plain and simple.

CRUSHER

Finn

And then I saw him—a young guy wearing what BB-8 said was his master's flight jacket.

I caught him and put him on the ground with my staff—I've never had much patience with thieves. He started babbling that BB-8's master was dead, that his name was Finn, and he was part of the Resistance, too. He also said BB-8 was carrying a map that would reveal the location of Luke Skywalker.

I didn't know who that was, which everybody thought was crazy.

On another day we might have had a galactic history lesson there in the Niima marketplace, but then the new arrivals showed up—First Order stormtroopers. They were shooting to kill, and they had TIEs flying cover.

We had to get as far away from Niima as quickly as possible. So I figured we'd steal the quad-jumper that Unkar kept insisting he was about to buy but never did—I'd flown a quad on my simulator. Great plan until the TIE pilots blew the quad up, forcing us to run for this junky freighter that the Blobfish has kept under a tarp for longer than I can remember.

I didn't think the thing would fly, but somehow it did. Finn got in the gun turret while BB-8 beeped his little head off and I tried to figure out somewhere we could lose the TIEs.

I headed for the Graveyard and the skeleton of that massive Super Star Destroyer—it was hollowed out and I knew I could maneuver in there, and I figured the one remaining pilot chasing us wouldn't know that.

Turns out I was right—Finn shot down the fighter and we headed for space. Unkar's freighter had red lights all over her console but she was a lot more maneuverable than I'd guessed, and really _fast_.

First Order
Stormtroopers

The
FALCON

Unfortunately, she was also falling apart—
shockingly enough, the Blobfish hadn't maintained
her properly. I figured out why she wasn't running
properly and was able to fix the problem—an
energy flux in the hyperdrive motivator caused a
fuel backup, rupturing a juncture in the auxiliary
system's trunking. See what I meant about the
importance of knowing your schematics?

After I got the ship fixed, I told Finn and BB-8 I'd
drop them at Ponemah Terminal, before going back
to Jakku. I knew the First Order was looking for
BB-8, and once he was gone they wouldn't care
about Jakku. I figured I could make things right
with the Blobfish by promising to fix everything
that was wrong with his freighter.

And if my people came back to Jakku and I was gone, they'd never find me again.

That was the plan, but then a huge bulk freighter swallowed us up. For a moment I figured it had to be Unkar, but it was a Wookiee called **Chewbacca** and an old Corellian named **Han Solo**. They said this had been their ship, and she was called the <u>Millennium Falcon</u>.

I'd heard of Chewbacca from some Wookiee traders who'd stopped off at Jakku. They said he was an amazing hyperspace scout and smart smuggler, with a reckless human first mate who was always getting him in trouble. I never dreamed I'd get to meet them.

Chewbacca and Solo

Han and Chewie had their own troubles—we barely had been introduced when some old friends of theirs caught up with us. There was a huge fight aboard the freighter, one that I spent trying not to get shot or torn apart by tentacles. We escaped in the Falcon, using this incredibly dangerous hyperspace maneuver I have to get Solo to explain to me if we ever get a minute of peace.

I've got to stop writing and get up to the cockpit. Our next stop is Takodana, where we're going to talk to an old friend of Chewie's named Maz.

I took a peek at Takodana on the scopes, and it looks like the planets I've dreamed about since I was a kid. Except even in my dreams they weren't _this_ green.

I wonder what we'll find down there....

Writer: Jason Fry
Editor: Amy Nathanson Heaslip
Art Director, Designer, and Illustrator: Andrew Barthelmes
Page Layout: Rebecca Stone
Copy Editor: Nancee Adams-Taylor
Managing Editor: Christine Guido
Creative Director: Julia Sabbagh
Associate Publisher: Rosanne McManus
Lucasfilm Editor: Frank Parisi
Lucasfilm Story Group: Leland Chee, Pablo Hidalgo, Rayne Roberts

Published by Studio Fun International, Inc.
44 South Broadway, White Plains, NY 10601 U.S.A. and
Studio Fun International Limited,
The Ice House, 124-126 Walcot Street, Bath UK BA1 5BG
All rights reserved. Studio Fun Books is a trademark
of Studio Fun International, Inc., a subsidiary of
The Reader's Digest Association, Inc.
Printed in the United States of America.
Conforms to ASTM F963 and EN 71
10 9 8 7 6 5 4 3 2 1